Aunt Flossie's Hats
(and Crab Cakes Later)

Aunt Flossie's Hats
(and Crab Cakes Later)

by Elizabeth Fitzgerald Howard

Paintings by James Ransome

CLARION BOOKS

New York

On Sunday afternoons, Sarah and I
go to see Great-great-aunt Flossie.
Sarah and I love Aunt Flossie's house.
It is crowded full of stuff and things.
Books and pictures and lamps and pillows…

Plates and trays and old dried flowers…
And boxes
and boxes
and boxes
of HATS!

On Sunday afternoons when Sarah and I
go to see Aunt Flossie, she says,
"Come in, Susan. Come in, Sarah.
Have some tea. Have some cookies.
Later we can get some crab cakes!"

We sip our tea and eat our cookies,
and then Aunt Flossie lets us look
in her hatboxes.

We pick out hats and try them on.
Aunt Flossie says they are her memories,
and each hat has its story.

Hats, hats, hats, hats!
A stiff black one with bright red ribbons.
A soft brown one with silver buttons.
Thin floppy hats that hide our eyes.
Green or blue or pink or purple.
Some have fur and some have feathers.
Look! This hat is just one smooth soft rose,
but here's one with a trillion flowers!
Aunt Flossie has so many hats!

One Sunday afternoon, I picked out
a wooly winter hat, sort of green, maybe.
Aunt Flossie thought a minute.
Aunt Flossie almost always thinks a minute
before she starts a hat story.
Then she sniffed the wooly hat.
"Just a little smoky smell now," she said.
Sarah and I sniffed the hat, too.
"Smoky smell, Aunt Flossie?"

"The big fire," Aunt Flossie said.
"The big fire in Baltimore.
Everything smelled of smoke for miles around.
For days and days.
Big fire. Didn't come near our house
on Centre Street, but we could hear
fire engines racing down St. Paul.

Horses' hooves clattering.
Bells! Whistles!
Your great-grandma and I couldn't sleep.
We grabbed our coats and hats and ran outside.
Worried about Uncle Jimmy's grocery store,
worried about the terrapins and crabs.
Big fire in Baltimore."

Aunt Flossie closed her eyes.
I think she was seeing long ago.
I wondered about crab cakes.
Did they have crab cakes way back then?
Then Sarah sniffed Aunt Flossie's hat.
"No more smoky smell," she said.
But I thought I could smell some,
just a little.

Then Sarah tried a different hat.
Dark, dark blue, with a red feather.
"This one, Aunt Flossie! This one!"
Aunt Flossie closed her eyes and thought a minute.
"Oh my, yes, my, my. What an exciting day!"

We waited, Sarah and I.
"What happened, Aunt Flossie?" I asked.

"Big parade in Baltimore."

"Ooh! Parade!" said Sarah. "We love parades."

"I made that hat," Aunt Flossie said,
"to wear to watch that big parade.
 Buglers bugling. Drummers drumming.

Flags flying everywhere. The boys—
soldiers, you know—back from France.
Marching up Charles Street. Proud.
Everyone cheering, everyone shouting!
The Great War was over!
The Great War was over!"

"Let's have a parade!" I said.
Sarah put on the dark blue hat.
I found a red one with a furry pompom.
We marched around Aunt Flossie's house.

"March with us, Aunt Flossie!" I called.
But she was closing her eyes.
She was seeing long ago.
"Maybe she's dreaming about crab cakes," Sarah said.

Then we looked in the very special box.
"Look, Aunt Flossie! Here's your special hat."
It was the big straw hat
with the pink and yellow flowers
and green velvet ribbon.
Aunt Flossie's favorite best Sunday hat!
It's our favorite story,
because we are in the story,
and we can help Aunt Flossie tell it!

Aunt Flossie smiled.
"One Sunday afternoon," she said,
"we were going out for crab cakes.
Sarah and Susan..."
"And Mommy and Daddy," I said.
"And Aunt Flossie," said Sarah.
Aunt Flossie nodded. "We were walking
by the water. And the wind came."

"Let me tell it," I said. "The wind came
and blew away your favorite best Sunday hat!"
"My favorite best Sunday hat," said Aunt Flossie.
"It landed in the water."
"It was funny," said Sarah.
"I didn't think so," said Aunt Flossie.

"And Daddy tried to reach it," I said, "but he slid down in the mud. Daddy looked really surprised, and everybody laughed." "He couldn't rescue my favorite, favorite best Sunday hat," said Aunt Flossie.

"And Mommy got a stick and leaned far out. She almost fell in, but she couldn't reach it either. The water rippled, and your favorite best Sunday hat just floated by like a boat!"

"Now comes the best part, and I'll tell it!"
said Sarah. "A big brown dog came.
It was walking with a boy.
'May we help you?' the boy asked.
'My dog Gretchen can get it.'
The boy threw a small, small stone.
It landed in Aunt Flossie's hat!
'Fetch, Gretchen, fetch!
Fetch, Gretchen, fetch!'

Gretchen jumped into the water
and she swam. She swam and she got it!
Gretchen got Aunt Flossie's hat!
'Hurray for Gretchen!'
We all jumped up and down.
'Hurray for Aunt Flossie's hat!'"

"It was very wet," said Aunt Flossie,
"but it dried just fine...almost like new.
My favorite, favorite best Sunday hat."

"I like that story," I said.
"So do I," said Sarah.
"And I like what happened next!
We went to get crab cakes!"

"Crab cakes!" said Aunt Flossie.
"What a wonderful idea! Sarah, Susan,
telephone your parents.
We'll go get some crab cakes right now!"

I think Sarah and I will always agree
about one thing: Nothing in the whole wide
world tastes as good as crab cakes.

But crab cakes taste best after stories…
stories about Aunt Flossie's hats!

To Lon (rock and sugar lump),
to Sarah and Jonathan (honey buns),
and in loving memory of Aunt Flossie.
—E.F.H.

To my mother Arsine,
thanks for all of your love and support.
—J.R.

Oil paints on canvas were used to create the full-color art in this book.
The text type is 14 pt. Galliard.

Clarion Books
a Houghton Mifflin Company imprint
215 Park Avenue South, New York, NY 10003
Text copyright © 1991 by Elizabeth Fitzgerald Howard
Illustrations copyright © 1991 by James Ransome
All rights reserved.
For information about permission to reproduce
selections from this book, write to Permissions,
Houghton Mifflin Company,
215 Park Avenue South, New York, NY 10003.
Printed in the USA

Library of Congress Cataloging-in-Publication Data
Howard, Elizabeth Fitzgerald.
Aunt Flossie's hats (and crab cakes later) / by Elizabeth
Fitzgerald Howard ; illustrated by James Ransome.
p. cm.
Summary: Sarah and Susan share tea, cookies, crab cakes, and
stories about hats when they visit their favorite relative, Aunt
Flossie.
ISBN 0-395-54682-6   PA ISBN 0-395-72077-X
[1. Hats—Fiction. 2. Great-aunts—Fiction. 3. Baltimore (Md.)—
Fiction.] I. Ransome, James, ill. II. Title.
PZ7.H83273Au 1990
[E]—dc20   90-33332
CIP
AC

B V G   20 19 18 17 16 15